THE FIRST TULIPS IN HOLLAND

THE FIRST TULIPS IN HOLLAND

BY PHYLLIS KRASILOVSKY

PICTURES BY S. D. SCHINDLER

Doubleday & Company, Inc. Garden City, New York

To my son Peter, my erstwhile traveling companion in Holland

Library of Congress Catalog Card Number 81-43109
Library of Congress Cataloging in Publication Data

Krasilovsky, Phyllis.
The first tulips in Holland.

Summary: A fictionalized account of how a Dutch merchant brought tulip bulbs from Persia to Holland where they became immensely popular.
[1. Tulips—Fiction. 2. Netherlands—Fiction]
I. Schindler, S. D. II. Title.
PZ7.K865Fi [E]
AACR2
ISBN: 0-385-17463-2 Trade
ISBN: 0-385-17464-0 Prebound

Printed in the United States of America
First Edition

Most people think
that tulips have
always grown
in Holland,
but that is not true.

Tulips first grew in a country called Persia many, many years ago. There they were admired by a Dutch visitor named Hendrik. No one knew the name of the flowers, so Hendrik called them tulips. Tulip is the Turkish word for turban, which is a sort of hat he noticed Persian men wearing. They looked as if they were the same shape to him.

Hendrik brought some tulip bulbs home to Holland as a present for his daughter, Katrina. She planted them in pebbles and water in a big blue bowl and put the bowl in the front window, where it would get the most sunlight.

After a few weeks, little green shoots came up through the pebbles. Soon they grew taller.

Naturally, since the bowl was in the front window, many people saw it when they passed the house. Everyone became interested in watching the green shoots grow day by day, especially since it was winter and the city was gray and drab.

Katrina watered the shoots every morning, and each time she did so, a nice young man, who was on his way to work, smiled at her. By the time the shoots had stems and had grown small green buds on top, Katrina had begun to smile back at him, and soon they were waving to each other as well.

When the buds grew bigger, more people stopped to stare into the window. No one had ever seen such plants before, and they were curious to see what they would look like when they bloomed.

Just before spring, the first bud opened into a lovely red tulip.

A few days later, there was suddenly a yellow one, and the next day, a purple one.

Soon all the tulips bloomed.
When they bloomed,
they got taller.

Now the word spread throughout the city
about the wonderful tulips.

Merchants came,

housewives came,

doctors and lawyers

and students and

officials came.

EVERYBODY came.

Even the great Prince of Orange came to see the tulips.

When Hendrik's neighbor saw how famous Hendrik had become because of the tulips, he offered him money to sell him one, but Hendrik refused.

Another neighbor offered him some hand-carved furniture for a single tulip, but Hendrik refused that as well.

One morning, when Henrik saw the prince looking into his window, admiring a new white tulip, he came out of his house and offered to give him a bulb.

It will bloom for you next spring, Sire," he said.

"How extraordinary!" the prince exclaimed.

"And it will multiply, so that in time you will have several tulips!" Hendrik said.

When the word spread that there would be tulips in the royal garden, everyone wanted one.

Complete strangers came to Henrik's door to offer him large sums of money and all kinds of gifts if he would part with a single bulb.

He was offered new horses for his carriage,

and fine jewelry for his wife,

a harpsichord,

even a herd of cows
and a flock of geese!

But each time, Hendrik refused.

After the flowers had withered away, Katrina took the blue bowl out of the window.

Now the nice young man couldn't wave to Katrina every morning anymore, and he missed her. Katrina missed him too. Sometimes she would peek through the window to see if he was passing by.

One day, the young man knocked on the door and asked Hendrik for his daughter's hand in marriage. When Hendrik saw that Katrina loved him, he asked, "How will you provide for her?"

The young man, whose name was Hans, said, "I grow flowers and sell them."

"In fact, I first noticed your daughter because of the way she watered the tulips so carefully each morning!" Since Hans was a florist, Henrik gave Katrina a dowry of tulip bulbs. Hans knew how to care for them, and within a few years, they had multiplied by the hundreds.

In time, he grew so many that each spring his garden looked like a brightly colored striped carpet. There were tulips of every color and kind. There were so many varieties that it was hard to choose the prettiest.

Now there were enough tulips for everyone. There were even enough to sell to people in other countries. Tulips soon became well known all over the world as Dutch flowers.

Today, everyone who visits Holland in the springtime can see a bowl of tulips in the front window of every house, and a bed of tulips in every garden, no matter how large or how small it is.

Afterword

The story you have just read is actually a fictionalized account of the way tulips appeared in Holland. In writing the story, I have tried to imagine how this beautiful flower might have influenced the lives of the people who loved it.

The very first tulips in the world appeared in the Middle East about four hundred years ago. They were grown to please a Turkish ruler who thought the flower so special that he passed strict laws forbidding the sale of tulips anywhere else. Nevertheless, a visitor to the country managed to send some bulbs to a friend in Czechoslovakia.

This friend was in charge of a huge public garden known as the Royal Medicinal Garden, and so of course he planted some bulbs there. Later he moved to Holland and took some bulbs with him. There he planted them in the botanical gardens in Leiden. Visitors to the gardens thought the tulips were beautiful and wanted to buy some, but he refused to sell any. One night, robbers sneaked into the gardens and stole many of the tulip bulbs. After that, people in all sorts of places managed to get them.

It was in Holland, though, that tulips originally flourished, grew popular, and eventually became known to the rest of the world as "the Dutch flower." The rest of of the tulip history is still a mystery, but it is true that a single tulip bulb was once worth the price of an entire house or a diamond ring. And merchants such as Hendrik played an important part in bringing tulips to their own villages in Holland.

— *Phyllis Krasilovsky*

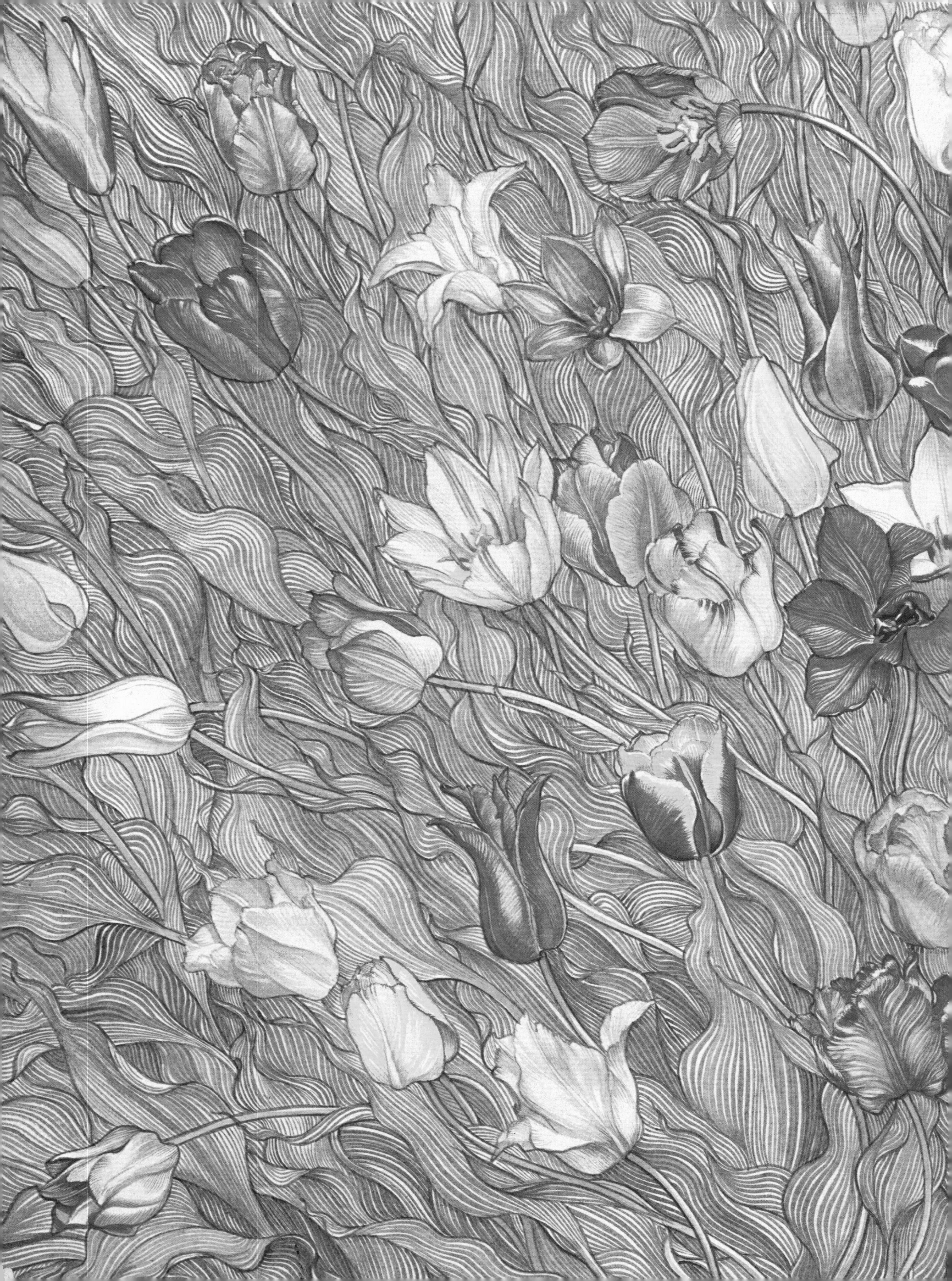